DISNEP · PIXAR

Cars

TRACTOR TROUBLE

By Frank Berrios

A GOLDEN BOOK • NEW YORK

www.randomhouse.com/kids

ISBN: 978-0-7364-2831-6

Printed in the United States of America

20 19 18 17 16 15 14 13 12

After a long day of **racing** practice, Lightning McQueen wanted to cool his engines **and relax**. But his best friend, Mater, had other plans.

"Let's go tractor tipping!" cried Mater.

The rusty tow truck quietly snuck up on two sleeping tractors and honked his horn.

HONK!

The startled tractors tipped back onto their large rear tires.

"I don't think this is a good idea," Lightning warned Mater. "You'll wake up Frank."

Suddenly, they heard a loud engine **ROAR** in the distance.

"Now you've done it," said Lightning.

Mater took off as Frank the combine started chasing him. Mater drove through the gate to make his escape, but his hook got caught and **ripped up** a section of the fence!

Frank **chased** Lightning and Mater toward town. The two friends ducked behind the new racetrack, and Frank drove right by. When the coast was clear, Lightning and Mater headed for home.

"This street feels soft and squishy," said Mater, looking down at his tires.

"Yeah," agreed Lightning. "It's **sticky,** too!"

"**Oh, no**—wet asphalt!" cried Lightning, looking at their tire tracks in the road. "I forgot they were paving this street today!"

"It doesn't look that bad," said Mater. "Maybe no one will notice our tracks."

But the next morning, Doc did notice the tracks—
and he wasn't happy!

"Mater and I forgot that the road to the new
racetrack was being paved yesterday," Lightning told
Doc. "What can we do to **fix** it?"

"You've got a race to get ready for, Lightning," said Mater, hooking himself up to Bessie. "I'll fix the road while you practice."

"Thanks!" replied Lightning. "You're the **best friend** a car could have!"

By the end of the day, Mater had finished repairing the road. **"Well done,"** said Doc. "But now I have another job for you. Do you think you can fix Frank's fence before those tractors get loose?"

"Sure can!" said Mater, and he **spun around** and drove off to fix the broken fence.

But fixing the fence was hard work, and Mater decided to take a nap before he was finished.

While Mater was asleep, the tractors rolled right through the broken fence and slowly **wandered off** in every direction.

The next day, Lightning went to check on Mater.

"Where are all the tractors, Mater?" asked Lightning.

"They were sitting right here last night," Mater said.

"We'd better round them up before they start causing **trouble,**" said Lightning.

Back in town, the tractors had made a **mess** of the new road.

"Mater, did you let the tractors out?" asked Sheriff.

"No, they kinda let themselves out," mumbled Mater.

"The road will never be ready in time for tomorrow's race!" cried Sally.

Mater felt **horrible**! He knew he had to fix the road again before all the race cars arrived.

"I'll get 'er done, even if I have to work all night," said Mater.

"If I help, you won't have to work all night," said Lightning.

"You need to **practice** for tomorrow's race," replied Mater.

"Pulling Bessie is great practice," said Lightning.

The next day, cars from all over arrived for the race. The town was buzzing with **excitement.** And more importantly, the road to the new racetrack was as smooth as glass. Lightning and Mater had done a fine job.

All of Lightning McQueen's friends lined up to watch the race. But where was Mater?

Silly Mater! He had brought all the tractors to see the race!

"You go get 'em, Lightning," yelled Mater. "Make 'em eat your dust!"

Lightning smiled and revved his engine. When the green flag was waved, Lightning zoomed off and quickly took the lead.

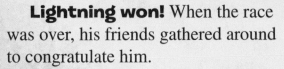

Lightning won! When the race was over, his friends gathered around to congratulate him.

"Pulling Bessie sure was a great way to warm up," Lightning told Mater.

"I brought along the tractors to **cheer** you on," said Mater. "I figured I could keep one eye on the tractors and the other eye on the race."

"Mater, you're a genius," Lightning replied with a smile.

"Now let's get those tractors back to Frank before he realizes they're missing," said Lightning.

"You betcha!" answered Mater. "Here, tractor, tractor, tractor! Follow the **shiny trophy**!"